Ike

Bakes a Cake

Written & Illustrated by Regina Dahl

WestBow Press books may be ordered through booksellers or by contacting:

WestBow Press
A Division of Thomas Nelson & Zondervan
1663 Liberty Drive
Bloomington, IN 47403
www.westbowpress.com
844-714-3454

Written & Illustrated by Regina Dahl

ISBN: 978-1-6642-3463-5 (sc)
ISBN: 978-1-6642-3464-2 (e)

Library of Congress Control Number: 2021909812

Print information available on the last page.

WestBow Press rev. date: 05/14/2021

WESTBOW
PRESS®
A DIVISION OF THOMAS NELSON
& ZONDERVAN

Ike puts on an apron.
This could be a mess!
What is Ike making?
Can you guess?

He uses some pans
to make something round.

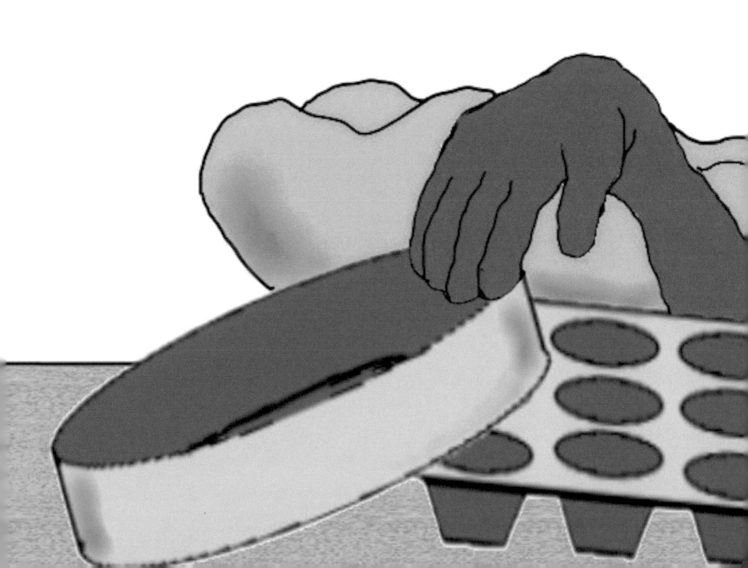

The ingredients are butter
and sugar, too.
Along with water and oil,
to name just a few.

He creams together the
butter and the sugar.
Baking can be so much fun!
Ike and his friends will celebrate,
when the work is done.

Mix and mix.
Stir and stir.
Oh, his friend will
like it, for sure!

The last ingredient—
in goes the flour!
Then, it is put into the oven
to bake for half an hour.

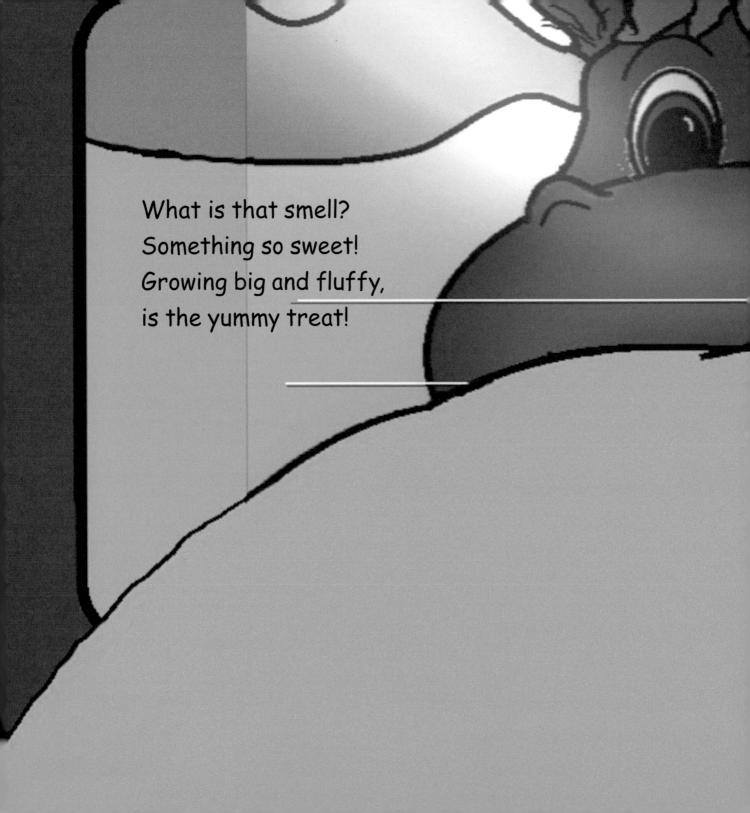

What is that smell?
Something so sweet!
Growing big and fluffy,
is the yummy treat!

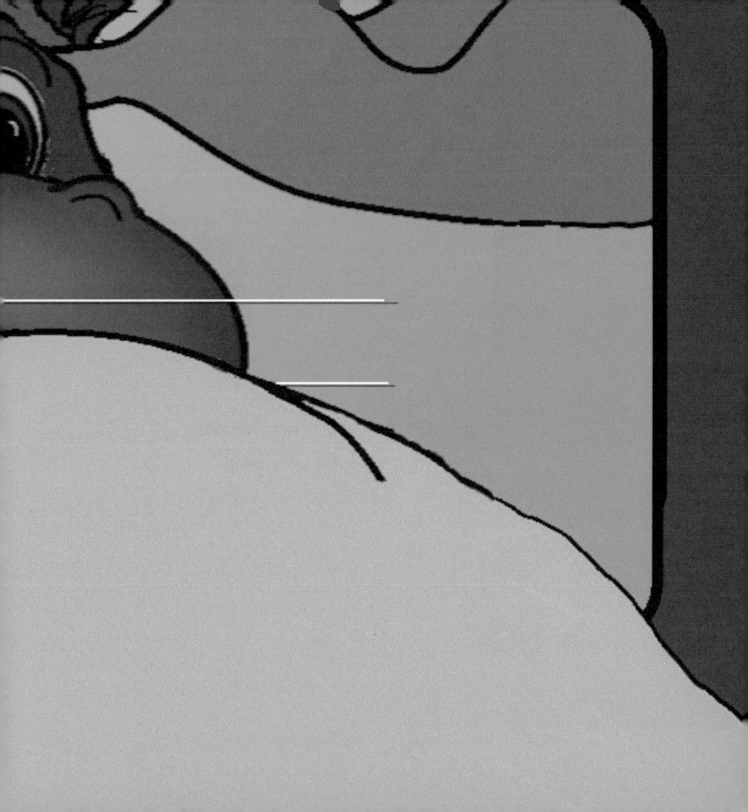

Time for the party!
Oh, what a surprise!
You could tell she was thrilled
by the size of her eyes!

What did she see?
What did Ike make?

Of course, now you know!
It was Abby's birthday cake!

Happy birthday, Abby!

Printed in the United States
by Baker & Taylor Publisher Services